DrRoach

D1395958

First published in Great Britain in 2014 by Boxer® Books Limited.

First published in the USA in 2014 by Boxer® Books Limited.

www.boxerbooks.com

Boxer® is a registered trademark of Boxer Books Limited.

Based on an original idea by Sam Williams.

Monstrous Stories™ concept, names, stories, designs and logos
© Boxer Books Limited

Written by Paul Harrison
Paul Harrison asserts his moral right to be identified
as the author of this work.
Text copyright © 2014 Boxer Books Limited

Illustrated by Tom Knight
Tom Knight asserts his moral right to be identified
as the illustrator of this work.
Illustrations copyright © 2014 Tom Knight

The illustrations were prepared using brush, ink and digital.
The text is set in Blackmoor Plain and Adobe Caslon.

ISBN 978 1 9079 6780 1
1 3 5 7 9 10 8 6 4 2

Printed in Great Britain

All of our papers are sourced from
managed forests and renewable resources.

Dr Roach's Monstrous STORIES

Dr Roach presents

PLANET OF THE GRAPES

a Boxer® Books production

Contents

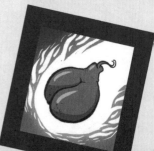

Dr. Roach welcomes YOU!

Have you ever had a pet? Jenny has several – she loves roaches. And I agree. We are quite lovable! Unfortunately, her dad doesn't think so. He can't wait to exterminate all of us.

One night, some very irresponsible aliens dump their food waste on earth – with disastrous consequences. Imagine – people actually begin to turn into giant grapes. That's right – giant grapes!

How lucky then that Jenny's extraordinary pet roaches are here to save the world!

How, you ask? Come closer, my friend, and I'll tell you all about it.

Welcome to Dr. Roach's Monstrous Stories. Enjoy!

COCKROACHES!

Nasty, scuttling, scrabbling cockroaches.

EVERYWHERE!

Inside and out.

They hid under beds, crept into cupboards and skulked in corners. They popped up in biscuits, swam in the toilet and plagued the playgrounds. They were an absolute menace and Bedford Falls had been OVERRUN by them.

Bad news for the poor townsfolk, but excellent news for Mr Crawley, owner of Creepy Crawley's Pest Control company. It was his job to get rid of the cockroaches. He'd never been so busy, which made him very happy.

One person who wasn't so happy was Mr Crawley's daughter, Jenny. If your dad is a pest controller then the worst possible pet to have is cockroaches, right? But Jenny had tried rabbits and goldfish and they were just too boring. Cockroaches on the other hand were fun, easy to look after and ate just about anything.

"There you go," said Jenny, popping the last of the apple into her cockroach house.

"Hi Jenny, I'm home," called her dad.

Quick as a flash she gathered up her things and hid the cockroaches under her bed – just as her dad poked his head round her door.

"You all right?" he said. "You look a little flushed."

"Fine thanks. You're home early," Jenny replied.

"Yeah, I'm exhausted. There are loads of those pesky cockroaches everywhere. I'll get rid of them all eventually…"

"I hope not," thought Jenny. "Not all of them."

Chapter 2
In Outer Space

Meanwhile deep in outer space there was trouble brewing. A shabby-looking spaceship with paint peeling from its sides, spluttered its way through the solar system. It was the most clapped-out rust bucket in the nearest five galaxies. The Nurgians,

from the planet Nurg, never looked
after anything, and were known
throughout the universe for their
laziness.

The Nurg spaceship looked
bad and so did the pilots! They
were bloated, warty, slimy, sweaty
creatures, mould green in colour
and wearing heavily stained brown
uniforms.

Their ship came to a halt in the shadow of a large asteroid.

"This will do," said the Nurg captain. "Prepare to empty the garbage."

"Aren't you worried that we'll get caught?" asked the co-pilot. "It's totally against Intergalactic Trash Rule 229b (section iii) on the safe disposal of waste."

The captain thought for a moment, stared at the co-pilot with his five

evil eyes and said, "Nope! Imagine taking this load of rotting junk to a space tip!"

The Nurgians laughed loudly.

The co-pilot pulled a lever and all sorts of strange space food drifted out: spiky purple fruits, twisted yellow vegetables and one that was all massive and wobbly, like a huge green bottom.

The rocket engines backfired into life and the Nurgians were gone.

Unfortunately that part of space wasn't quite as empty as the Nurgians thought. Their garbage was being pulled towards a blue planet with swirling clouds: a planet we know as Earth!

Chapter 3
Nurgian Grape Juice

Jenny waited until her dad was asleep before she fed her cockroaches.
She slipped some more apple into their plastic cage and watched the cockroaches scrabble over it. They polished off the food in no time then scurried back to the dark corners.

Jenny went to bed, but she couldn't sleep. No matter which way she lay she just couldn't get comfy.

"Now I'm thirsty," she grumped and slouched downstairs to the kitchen.

As the water splashed into her glass she looked blearily out of the window. There were great streaks of light burning through the sky!

"Oh wow," said Jenny, "shooting stars!"

For the next few minutes the dark night sky was filled with brilliant lines of light that vanished almost as quickly as they appeared.

One was twice as big and twice as bright as any of the others and it sped past like it was heading right over the town.

"Hah! That one looked like a massive green bottom!" said Jenny. "I must be tired; I'm seeing things now."

She yawned and made her way to bed.

As it happened she hadn't been seeing things. That was no ordinary shower of shooting stars – it was the Nurgian rubbish burning up in the Earth's atmosphere. And the backside-shaped shooting star was

actually a giant Nurgian Splurge
grape. It was much too big to burn
up completely; instead it plummeted
towards Bedford Falls and landed
with a massive

KER-SPLAT

in the middle of the town square.
   Nurgian grape juice was everywhere
and slowly dribbled into the ground.

Chapter 4
Grape Invasion!

Jenny woke the next morning and opened her bedroom curtains.

"DAD! What kind of plant grows the height of a house overnight?" she shouted.

"I don't know, honey," Mr Crawley asked sleepily. "Why?"

"Because there's one outside my window!" said Jenny.

Her dad peered at the mass of vegetation.

"Where did it come from?" asked Jenny.

"Out of the ground I suppose," said her dad.

"I know that!" said Jenny as she squeezed past the thick stem of the plant by the front door.

"Whoa, it's massive!"

"I hope there's not a giant up there," her dad mumbled.

"Look, it's got fruit on it," said Jenny. "They look like grapes – yuck. I can't stand grapes!"

"Grapes – ooh I love grapes," said her dad, popping one in his mouth.

"Dad, you don't know what they are! They might be poisonous!" shouted Jenny.

"Nope, they're definitely grapes.
In fact, no, they're not just grapes –
they're the best grapes ever."

"Hey, have you tried those grapes?"

shouted Mr Jenks, the neighbour.
"They're delicious!"

"But Mr Jenks," pleaded Jenny,
"you're from the council – shouldn't
we be testing them or something? I
mean it's a bit strange how they've
just appeared overnight."

Mr. Jenks just smiled.

"Nah, I'm sure they're fine. Anyway can't stop – I'll be late for work!"

"Me too, gotta dash," said Mr. Crawley. "I'll take some of these for the journey."

He picked some more grapes.

"Here try one!"

He threw one to Jenny and went upstairs to get ready.

Jenny went to her room and dropped the grape into the cockroach house.

"Hmm, even you seem to like them," she said as her pets swarmed over the fruit. "But I'm not so sure – I'm going to chop that plant down. There's something about it I just don't like."

When Jenny opened her front door the next morning, she couldn't believe what she was seeing.

"Dad, that plant is in front of our door!" said Jenny.

"Well it was there yesterday, so where else did you expect it to be? It's not like it can walk," her dad replied.

"No, I cut it down yesterday," said Jenny. "And now it's grown back and it's bigger than before!"

"You cut it down!" he replied. "But why?"

He plucked a couple of grapes and popped them into his mouth.

When Mr Crawley eventually managed to push past the plant outside the front door and over the branches growing across the path he discovered that the garage and his van were completely covered in vines.

For a moment he looked absolutely flabbergasted, but then he just shrugged his shoulders.

"The walk will do me good," he said.

Jenny watched open-mouthed. Normally her dad got angry if his cereal was soggy, but now he was whistling his way to work without a care in the world. Jenny looked

down the street. There were vines
everywhere – twisted around
lampposts, pushing into drains,
covering cars and wrapping round
the roofs of buildings.

"This is ridiculous!" said Jenny.
"Why isn't anybody doing anything
about this? Can't they see what's
happening? Well if no one else will
do something I will."

Still in her pyjamas she marched to the garage and managed to climb through a window. Inside the garage were the weed killers and other dangerous stuff she was absolutely forbidden from using.

"Ultra Killer Weed Remover – see results INSTANTLY. That's the one!" said Jenny.

Half an hour later Jenny had covered every vine around the house. And then she waited. And she waited.

"Nothing! It did nothing!" she said. "But that's impossible – just what are they?"

Then Jenny remembered the strange green shooting star. The grapes on this plant looked like small versions of it … she started to get really worried.

Chapter 6
Emergency!

Jenny looked up and down the street. People couldn't get into their cars or on their bikes – but no one seemed to mind! Everywhere people were laughing and smiling, chatting to complete strangers and popping the grapes into their mouths without a care in the world … everyone was impossibly happy.

"That's it!" cried Jenny. "It's got to be the grapes. Everyone's acting strangely – except for me. The only reason I'm not acting weird is I've not been eating them."

Then a thought struck her – what about her cockroaches? She'd been feeding them the grapes – had they been affected? She dashed upstairs and checked; they seemed as lively

and as normal as ever … except there were more of them – a lot more of them. Was that because of the grapes too?

FLUMP!

"What was that noise?" thought Jenny.

FLUMP!

FLUMP!

FLUMP!
FLUMP!
FLUMP!

FLUMPFLUMPFLUMP
FLUMPFLUMPFLUMP
FLUMPFLUMPFLUMP
FLUMPFLUMPFLUMP!

Jenny stared out of her window in disbelief. All the grapes were suddenly expanding in size. They were gigantic now – easily as big as a person! She needed her dad and she needed him now!

"Hi Jenny, what are you doing here?" asked Mr Crawley as Jenny burst into his office.

"Dad, look at the grapes!" shouted Jenny.

"Oh Jenny, you need to relax about the … oh that felt odd," he replied.

"Dad – you're turning green!" cried Jenny.

"I don't feel very well," wailed Mr Crawley.

"DAD! You're starting to swell up!"

Mr Crawley was changing. First his face and hands went all puffy and then his body began to expand like a balloon.

"Dad, you look like an enormous grape!" shrieked Jenny. "We need to get you to the hospital – and fast!"

The only way Jenny could move her father was by rolling him along the road. When she eventually got to the hospital she was in for another surprise. The whole building was filled with people who looked like human grapes!

Chapter 7
To The Rescue

Jenny stared at the half-human, half-grapes that rolled around her.

"The whole town has been turned into homo-grapians!" she said. "I must be the only one left who hasn't been infected with whatever it is in that fruit! What do I do now?"

The situation was getting worse. The vines were spreading everywhere – Jenny had to warn the neighbouring towns and get some help!

CRACKLE! FIZZ! POP!

The weight of the huge grapes was pulling down all the telephone wires, electricity cables and radio masts. No phones. No internet. And Jenny couldn't even cycle out of town. The grapes had taken over!

"Well I can't get help so it looks like it's up to me to do something about these pesky plants on my own. But what? I've tried cutting them down and poisoning them, but that doesn't work … Hold on a sec! I wonder … Dad, don't roll off anywhere, I'll be back in a minute!"

Jenny raced home and got her pet cockroaches. As she suspected they

were as lively as ever and there were
even more of them than last time.

"OK my beauties, you know how
you like the taste of those grapes?
Well you can stuff your faces as
much as you like!"

With that she emptied the
cockroaches all over the vine outside
her front door. For a moment
her pets did nothing – then they

suddenly started attacking the plants like they had been starved for a week.

The speed that the cockroaches managed to chomp their way through the vine surprised even Jenny. Within a couple of minutes the huge plant had been reduced to a couple of shredded bits of stem and leaves. More importantly it was showing no sign of recovering.

"Way to go roaches!" shouted Jenny. "You must be getting the roots too!"

What was just as remarkable was that the more the cockroaches ate, the quicker they began to breed. After five minutes there was double the number of cockroaches that

Jenny had emptied out from her tank. And to top it all the more the cockroaches ate, the hungrier they seemed to get. Within an hour the hordes of cockroaches had cleared the vines completely.

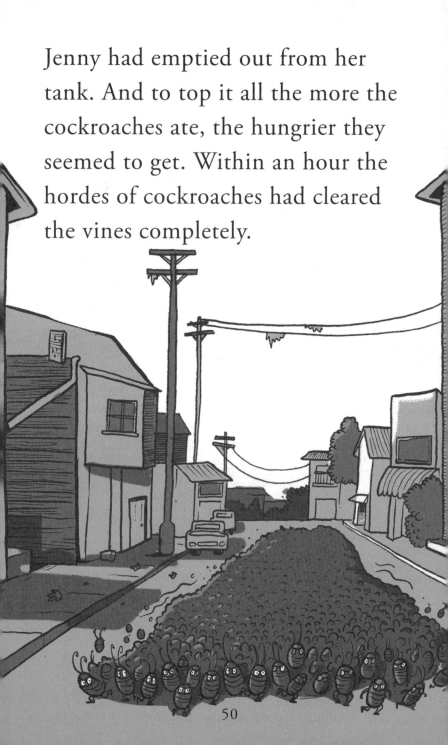

Jenny dashed to the hospital to tell her dad the good news.

"Excellent!" said her dad. "Now all we need is a cure for us."

He waved a chubby arm around at his fellow homo-grapians.

"Erm, I'm not so sure ..." said Jenny looking out of the window.

She could see thousands upon thousands of cockroaches all heading towards the hospital like a rolling brown wave.

"What's wrong?" asked Mr Crawley, waddling to the window.

"I think the cockroaches are still hungry," said Jenny.

"But all the grapes are gone, why are they coming here? It's not like we've got any!"

Jenny looked at her dad. He was big, green and nearly round – just like a human-sized grape.

"Dad, we've got to get you all out of here!! The cockroaches think you're food! Everybody – roll for it!"

And they did. They rolled down corridors, down stairwells and down laundry chutes – until they were finally all outside.

But the cockroaches were gaining.

"Please roll faster," Jenny pleaded.

And as they did something remarkable happened.

The more the people rolled, the less grape-like they looked.

"If we can just keep this up, we might get you all back to normal," shouted Jenny.

Disaster! Coming the other way up the road were more cockroaches, with demon-eyes, green and glowing! The townsfolk were surrounded!

"This is it," wailed Mr Crawley. "Eaten by cockroaches – and me a pest control officer!"

The cockroaches scuttled up to the frightened people and were about to pounce when:

POP!

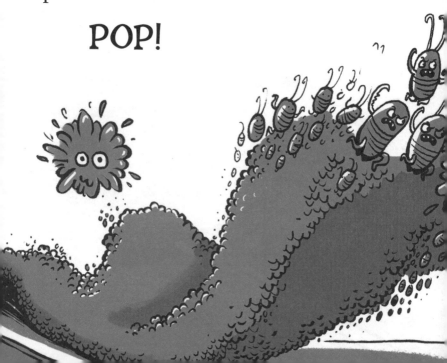

One of them exploded.

POP POP POP!

And then some more.

**POPPOPPOP
POPPOPPOP
POPPOP!**

"What's going on?" shouted Mr Crawley.

"Of course," cried Jenny. "The grapes are making the roaches expand as well but their hard bodies won't let them grow that quick!"

With one final mighty explosion the cockroaches blew up – showering the people in sticky roach juice.

"Saved!" shouted Jenny.

She'd never been so happy to be covered in bug guts – and it's not often you can say that.

After a week or so of rolling around the good people of Bedford Falls were back to normal again, though they never seemed to eat grapes any more. As for Jenny, well she decided that cockroaches weren't so great as pets after all. She'd try something less disgusting instead.

Like slugs.

Have you ever smelled a raccoon's gigantic bottom burp? Not for the squeamish, I can tell you. Raccoons can be rather cute really – unless they have been eating the wrong food.

One night, our greedy friend finds some rather tasty morsels that turn him into a crazy monster with laser-beam eyes set on destroying the town of Hummerfield in search of more food!

Luckily for the townsfolk, young Jimmy Schwartz is on the trail of the raccoon of doom and saves the day.

How, you ask? Get a copy today and I'll tell you everything!

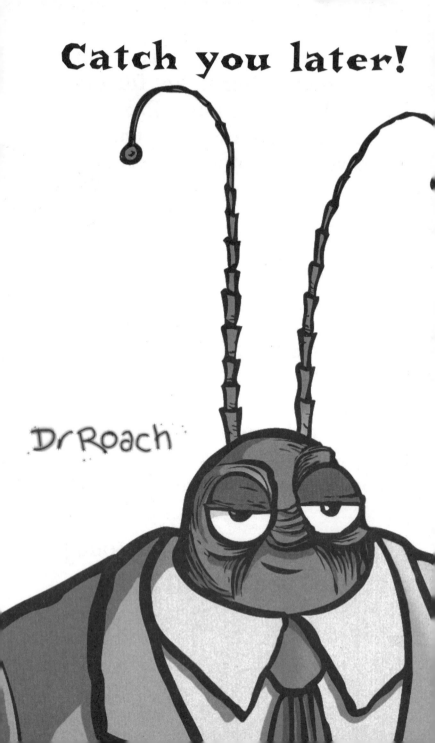